I See the Crowd Roar

I See the Crowd Roar

The Inspiring Story of William "Dummy" Hoy

Dr. Joseph C. Roetheli
and
Agnes Roetheli Gaertner

I See the Crowd Roar
© 2014 The Roetheli Lil' Red Foundation

All rights reserved. No part of this book may be reproduced in any form or by any means, electronic, mechanical, photocopying, scanning, or otherwise, without permission in writing from the publisher, except by a reviewer who may quote brief passages in a review. For information on licensing, permissions or special sales, contact the publisher at info@dunhamgroupinc.com.

978-1-939447-30-2 (Trade paperback)
978-1-939447-31-9 (ebook)

Printed in the United States of America

TABLE OF CONTENTS

A Note from the Publisher........................... 7

Preface 11

Introduction: A Winner 13

Chapter One: The Life and Times of
William "Dummy" Hoy 17

Chapter Two: The Origin of the Nickname "Dummy".... 27

Chapter Three: Hand Signals........................ 35

Chapter Four: It Takes Character 45

Chapter Five: A Cobbler's Life....................... 51

Chapter Six: The Road to Success 59

Chapter Seven: The Wonder Years 65

Chapter Eight: It's a Wonderful Life
after Major League Baseball......................... 73

Chapter Nine: The Great American Pastime—
Yesterday and Today................................ 79

Chapter Ten: The Great Debate of Cooperstown........ 87

Conclusion: Adversity Can be Your Friend 95

Appendices... 97

About the Authors................................. 103

A Note from the Publisher

Dr. Joseph Roetheli has had a successful career working for universities, the federal government, directing his own companies, and leading a charitable foundation (www.lilredfoundation.org). He and the co-author of this book, Agnes Roetheli Gaertner (who is also his sister), are fond of the fact that they had the opportunity to experience freedom, work hard, pull themselves up by the "bootstraps," and thus achieve the American Dream. Many people of the world do not have these opportunities, as we Americans do.

Dr. Roetheli never had the opportunity to play any organized ball, but Agnes played softball on a community team. However, their family did listen to nearly every St. Louis Cardinals' baseball game on the radio. Yes, radio, because the family had no TV, no central heat, and no air conditioning.

Today, one of Dr. Roetheli's major goals is to inspire people and to help young people become the best they can be despite challenges. This book is designed to help inspire young people by showing how one hearing and speech-impaired small man, William "Dummy" Hoy, faced immense hurdles and overcame them. William became one of the best Major League outfielders in the late 1800s. William had a dream and worked hard, practiced whenever he could, stayed focused, and lived as a CHARACTERED person.

Read this book to learn more about a CHARACTERED person from the Roethelis' perspective. You can't succeed by sitting on the sidelines or by complaining. You must focus on your talents, just as William Hoy did, and take a step forward toward your dream every day!

Serge Roetheli, the authors' distant Swiss relative, also had a dream: to run around the world. He accomplished this and many other feats by always staying focused on his goals. He achieved amazing feats in eight sports endurance categories and has been referred to as likely the greatest endurance athlete ever (www.the25000milelovestory.com). Serge says: "Anything is possible if you are willing to pay the price."

What price are you willing to pay to reach your dream?

Enjoy reading about William Hoy and learning from this book.

Work hard and become the very best you can be.

Pursue the American Dream! It is waiting for you, as it was for the Roethelis—and as it was for William Hoy!

—Dunham Books

William Hoy, record-setting center fielder.

Note: Photography in the latter half of the 1800s was just in its early stages of development. (Photography was invented in 1826.) Hence, the old photographs in this book are not of the high quality (resolution) that is common today.

Preface

Suppose you could not hear or you could not speak, and you were much smaller than most people. Would you have the courage and persistence to succeed in reaching your dream to play Major League baseball? William Hoy did. You can learn a great deal from him in this book.

Baseball great William "Dummy" Hoy became the first deaf player to have an extended career in the Major Leagues. He was a rookie in 1888. Fourteen years later, he played his last Major League game in 1902.

He dedicated much of the rest of his life to developing and encouraging young baseball players, especially those with physical challenges who were playing on community teams. William himself grew up playing street baseball outside his house with his friends and with local amateur teams. Using a little imagination and a lot of research about this baseball legend's inspiring story, we believe William "Dummy" Hoy was the type of person who might have defined a youth baseball league's purpose and primary objectives in the following way:

The Purpose of Youth Baseball

In every city and town in America, a youth baseball league should aspire to be an outstanding educational and athletic organization. It should provide a high quality experience. The young athletes should be provided the opportunity to learn, play, and enjoy the game of baseball in a wholesome community atmosphere.

The cornerstone of the league's purpose should be to help young people become the best individuals and citizens they can be. Its goal should be to help build positive self-esteem and good character in each young person. It should instill and foster teamwork, discipline, responsibility, loyalty, respect, friendship, tolerance, good sportsmanship, and a drive for excellence. It requires good coaching and quality instruction in a positive and enjoyable environment. All parents should be strongly encouraged to participate, along with their children, in this youth program. They should provide proper guidance and exemplary leadership in such volunteer positions as coaches, managers, umpires, and local league board members.

The youth baseball league should provide a fun, enjoyable experience, and it should serve as a positive influence in the lives of young baseball players across America. It should also improve the players' skills and knowledge of the game.

Introduction
A WINNER

There's an old saying that goes: "If you're aiming at nothing, you'll hit it every time." This means, if you never set a goal, you will achieve nothing. You will have no target to aim at. You will have nothing to strive for. You will not be a winner.

A winner is often defined as "the person or team with the best score." But in its basic form, what is a winner? Winning means much more than beating your opponent. Winners always put forth 100 percent effort. They push themselves to the very limit of their abilities. They overcome obstacles and disadvantages blocking their way. They are team players; they are respectful and honest. Winners show good sportsmanship. As Halle Berry once said: "When I was a kid, my mother told me that if you could not be a good loser, then there's no way you could be a good winner."

You can certainly be a winner without winning the game. You simply must perform at your full potential. On the flip side, if you beat your opponent by cheating or giving less than your best effort, then you can't be a real winner.

Throughout his life and baseball career, William "Dummy" Hoy became a winner against all odds. He set an "impossible dream" for himself. Well, it seemed impossible to many, including his own family. Even though William had been deaf since the age of three, his passion was to play professional baseball. He dreamed of a successful career in the Major Leagues.

And what is your dream?

William practiced long and hard for years. When he retired in 1902 after playing 1,797 games in the Major Leagues, William was certainly—by anybody's standard—a winner.

His hard work, his ethical beliefs, and his remarkable intelligence led him to be a true winner, both on and off the field. He even became an American hero to legions of admiring fans. They waved their hands, arms, and hats when William made a good play. He could not hear the crowd roar, but he could see them wave. Thus the title of this book—I See the Crowd Roar.

The Definition of a Winner

- A winner has a dream and the ambition to pursue that dream.
- A winner is motivated to work and practice hard.
- A winner is a team player; one who never plays just for himself or herself.
- A winner has discipline, always playing with focused determination and drive.

- A winner has a big heart full of integrity and character.
- A winner has a positive attitude and competes fairly.
- A winner works and plays with honor and respect.
- A winner has confidence in himself or herself.
- A winner has the inner courage and strength to endure adversity.
- A winner learns from life's lessons.

William (second from right in second row) with his parents and siblings.

Chapter One

THE LIFE AND TIMES OF WILLIAM "DUMMY" HOY

William Ellsworth Hoy was born on May 23, 1862. 1862: that's over 150 years ago. The Civil War was still raging at that time between the North and the South. Baseball was becoming more and more popular as a much-needed distraction from the War Between the States. So over the years, baseball's popularity increased, and baseball came to be known as the "Great American Pastime."

Life was very different in William Hoy's time. Let's consider some of these differences to help us understand how William grew up in the 1860s and 1870s.

Most homes in the latter half of the nineteenth century were heated with wood or coal fireplaces. Fireplaces were generally built with stones. The stones of the fireplace would hold heat and help warm the house. Individual heated stones were wrapped in a blanket and taken to bed to help keep you warm. Most beds were simply made of boards, often with no mattress.

There were no cars or airplanes for high-speed travel. William and his friends walked to each other's homes. Families rode in a horse-drawn buggy or a springboard wagon with wooden wheels. When there was snow on the ground, the people with more money might use a sleigh, drawn by horses. Most of these methods of travel were not enclosed. So, travel in winter was cold, with the wind always blowing in your face. Heated stones were often wrapped in a blanket and put under your feet to keep them warm while riding in a buggy, wagon, or sleigh. When traveling on foot or by a horse-drawn vehicle, the speed was generally less than five miles per hour. Trains, a relatively new mode of transportation, were used for longer trips, as they were considerably faster.

Towns were often seven to eight miles apart. A trip to town for a farmer and his family often required a full day. First, they had to harness the horses and load the wagon with farm goods to sell or trade. Then they would travel perhaps an hour and a half to get to town, shop at the general store, and then load the wagon with supplies. Finally, they would make the long trip back home.

Small towns typically had a church, a school, a general store, a carpentry shop, a blacksmith shop, and a cobbler's (shoe) shop, and not a lot more. The grocery section of the general store was typically small and stocked with just some select items. Candy was stored in a large barrel and being able to buy just one piece was a huge treat for farm children. Many people bought fruits, vegetables, and meat directly from local farmers.

Over 50% of the 3,929,000 people in the United States lived on farms when William Hoy was born. Today, there are over 312 million people in the United States, but only 4% live on farms and only about 2% are actually farmers. In the latter half of the 1800s, a high percentage of the population grew some of their own food in home gardens. They had to till the soil with a spade and prepare a seed bed, and then plant the seeds. After the plants sprouted, they would water the plants, hoe and weed the garden, and check for and remove bugs. In the summer and fall, they would harvest the crops.

Most doctors were not well trained by today's standards. There were very few doctors who were specialists. Modern medicines did not exist. For example, Alexander Fleming did not discover penicillin, the bacteria-killing drug, until 1928. In William's time, an illness often became fatal.

When William turned eighteen in 1890, there were only 47,900 telephones in the entire United States. Only seven out of every one thousand people had a phone. Most of the phones were in the cities, and hardly any farmers had phones.

Radios, televisions, and electronic games had not yet been invented. The first radio station began broadcasting in 1920, when William was already fifty-eight years old. The first TV station began broadcasting in Washington, DC, in 1928.

Today, Oklahoma, Kansas, and Nebraska aren't really that far away from William's birthplace in Ohio. But when William was born, those states were still considered part of the frontier. American Indians lived on the frontier and beyond. They harvested buffalo for food and clothing. Large herds of buffalo were still roaming across the Great Plains until after the cross-country railroad was completed in 1870.

> An excellent place to learn more about the life and times when William Hoy was growing up is the Steamboat Arabia Museum in Kansas City, Missouri. This museum is a time capsule of artifacts recovered from the sunken Steamboat Arabia, which was discovered in the late 1980s. In 1858, this boat

> was loaded with commonly used materials and then headed out of Kansas City to the frontier. The Steamboat Arabia sank just five miles up the Missouri River from Kansas City. At the museum, you can see rectangular nails, beaver hats, work boots, trapping gear, and a host of other items of that time. You might even get to see one of the jars of pickles dug up in the excavation! These pickles were still good to eat about 130 years after the boat sank. And you might learn why the pickles were so well preserved!

When William was ten years old, he was enrolled in the Ohio School for the Deaf. When it first opened in 1829, this school was called the Institute for the Education of the Deaf and Dumb. It was one of the first schools to educate children who could not hear or speak. Beginning in 1838, the school stressed sign language. That same year, trade shops (a shoe shop and a machine shop) run by private tradesmen were also opened. In 1870, just two years before William entered the school, the age for admission was lowered from twelve to ten years of age. That same year, lip reading was added to the studies. The students all lived on the school campus, because most of their homes were too far away to walk or ride a horse to school every day.

William was a very intelligent student, and he worked very hard. He finished his elementary and high school studies in just seven years. He learned shoe repair as a vocation at the Ohio School for the Deaf. At age seventeen, he graduated as the high school valedictorian (the best in his class).

While he was in school, he would practice throwing a ball against the brick wall at the school for hours at a time, and, as often as possible, to develop a powerful and accurate arm. (Did you know that studies show that to be great at almost anything requires about 10,000 hours of practice?) Over time, his throwing arm became strong and extremely accurate as a result of his practice.

After graduation, William worked on his father's farm. Then he went to work in a shoe repair shop, and finally he opened his own cobbler's shop. In his spare time, he always played baseball or practiced throwing.

Finally, at age twenty-four, he began his professional career in Oshkosh, Wisconsin. After two seasons there, he joined the Washington Senators, his first major-league team. William was an excellent base runner. By the end of his rookie year with the Senators, William led the National League in stolen bases—an astounding 82. No rookie was able to break this record for stolen bases for almost 100 years. (Vince Coleman, of the St. Louis Cardinals, finally broke Hoy's record in 1985). Hoy became one of the leading Major League base stealers of his day.

William's proudest memory, however, was a defensive play, using his strong and accurate throwing arm. He likely was the smallest Major League outfielder in history, but he was admired as a "flyhawk." As a speedy centerfielder, he threw out three base runners at home plate in one game on June 19, 1889. This is a rare feat for a player in any era. Although it has been tied twice, it is a record that still stands today, nearly 125 years after William's amazing performance on the field. His defensive ability was right up there with legends such as Joe DiMaggio and Willie Mays.

Another great day for William was May 1, 1901. On that day, he hit the second grand slam in the newly formed American League. (His teammate, Herm McFarland, had hit the first one earlier in the same game.) That year, he played in 130 games and hit .294 for the Chicago White Stockings and helped them win the first AL pennant. He had forty-five assists from the field—a record for any league.

His speed was his greatest asset, both defensively and offensively. He had a Major League career total of 596 stolen bases. Most of his forty home runs were inside the park homers, and he scored a whopping 1,429 runs during his fourteen years in the majors. That's an average of over 100 runs per season. And defensively, he had 328 assists and nearly 4,000 putouts as a centerfielder.

For eighteen seasons, William enjoyed a long and successful professional career. During fourteen of those years, he played 1,797 games in the Major Leagues. This was the most games played by any outfielder at the time. He also set the record for career putouts with 3,964. William played for four of the five Major Leagues of his day—the National League, the American League, the Players' League, and the original American Association. Very few players have played for teams in this many leagues.

After playing 1,797 games in the Major Leagues, William Hoy retired. He bought a sixty-acre dairy farm on the outskirts of Cincinnati and operated it for twenty years. He used his celebrity status to foster the needs and concerns of the deaf. During World War I, he was the personnel director of several hundred deaf workers at the Goodyear Tire Company. He coached the Goodyear Silents (the company baseball club) from 1919 to 1920. He also coached and umpired deaf-team games. He never lost his enthusiasm for baseball, nor his zest for life.

In 1951, William Dummy Hoy was unanimously voted the first player to be inducted into the Hall of Fame of the American Athletic Association of the Deaf. In 2003, he was inducted into the Cincinnati Reds Hall of Fame. The USA Deaf Sports Federation began lobbying to get William Hoy inducted into the National Baseball Hall of Fame in Cooperstown, New York, while he was still alive, and continues to do so today.

On October 7, 1961, at age ninety-nine, William Hoy tossed out the ceremonial first pitch of the third game of the World Series at Crosley Field (Reds vs. Yankees). Shortly afterwards, he became ill and was hospitalized. On December 15, 1961, he died of a stroke, just six months shy of his hundredth birthday.

* * * * *

In the following chapters of this book, you will discover more amazing details about this unsung hero of baseball. You will read interesting moments from his childhood and learn of his hard work to develop his playing skills. You will read about his record-breaking career and fascinating post-game life. You will be introduced to his beautiful wife and his children. You will learn about William's struggle to succeed and communicate in his silent world. You will learn to understand and admire his drive to become the best player he could be. You will learn more about why William Hoy was a *winner*. And you will learn how you can become a winner, too.

Chapter One Questions

1. When William was born in 1862, what historical event was happening in the nation?

2. What was the name of the special school that William attended?

3. What trade did William learn while attending school?

4. What was the name of the first ball club in the Major Leagues that signed William?

5. How many years did William play on professional baseball teams?

6. How many years did William play on Major League teams?

7. How did William develop such a strong and accurate throwing arm?

8. In his rookie year, William led the National League with how many stolen bases?

HOUCKTOWN

HOME OF
William "Dummy" Hoy
1862 - 1961
Member Ohio Baseball Hall of Fame

35 M.P.H.

Chapter Two
THE ORIGIN OF THE NICKNAME "DUMMY"

William was not born deaf. He could hear the birds chirping in the trees and his mother singing a lullaby until he was three years old. Then he came down with meningitis. Meningitis is a very serious disease. It is caused by a virus, and it inflames the membranes which protect the brain and the spinal cord. Even today, this disease can be life threatening. It must be treated immediately with antibiotics. But the doctors in William's time had no antibiotics, because they hadn't been discovered yet. Consequently, William became deaf and mute as a result of this disease. He was fortunate that he did not die, because meningitis was fatal for many children in William's era.

Because a deaf person can't hear, learning to speak is very difficult. There are different levels of deafness, but many deaf people don't hear well enough to copy the sounds of human speech. Therefore, they either don't speak at all or cannot be understood. In the nineteenth and early twentieth century, they were called either "dumb" or "mute"—which meant silent. It's very important to remember that William lived in a different time. Back then, being called "dumb" was not considered an insult the way it is now. It merely referred to the fact that a person could not speak. So, people who could not speak were often nicknamed "Dummy." The affectionate nickname "Dummy" was not considered a hurtful or negative insult.

Although William's legal name was William Ellsworth Hoy, he himself insisted that he be called by his nickname, "Dummy." William was by no means stupid. He overcame the fact that he could neither hear nor speak. He could read lips and often corrected people who used Bill or Will or William. Later, when he played professional baseball, he was usually listed in newspaper accounts and record books as Bill, Billy, William, or W. E., and only occasionally, as "Dummy."

Not only was William both deaf and unable to speak, but he was also a small man. He was only 5'4" tall, and only weighed somewhere between 145-155 pounds over his eighteen-year career (records differ on the exact numbers). Throughout his childhood, he was teased and bullied about his size and his deafness. Whenever his parents took him into town, other kids would make fun of him because of the odd squeaking sounds he made when he tried to speak. Many people probably broke "The Golden Rule" (treat others as you would want them to treat you) when meeting William. He was very shy, but he grew up building his character. He possessed a strong sense of self-worth by always believing in himself, his athletic abilities, and his baseball skills.

William's parents, who could hear, weren't sure how to help him. Few resources were available to people in such situations in the 1800s. They probably had questions such as: "How can we teach William to communicate at home?" "How can we help William make friends?" "Where should we send him to school?" or "What will his future be like?" Luckily, they found a special School for the Deaf in Columbus, Ohio. They enrolled William in this school, which was 100 miles from their home. William had to live at the school, because it took much longer at that time to travel 100 miles than it does today. (How long would it take you to walk or ride a horse 100 miles?)

Young William's hearing loss was severe. He was not able to speak, but he did learn to read lips on his own. This demonstrated how bright he was. William could only manage to utter sounds in what was described as mouse-like squeaks.

People back in the 1800s didn't really understand what it was like to be deaf. (And it's pretty much the same today.) Many people believed that just because deaf people couldn't hear or talk, they couldn't do other things. Therefore, William was put on the manual labor track at school. He was taught to be a cobbler (a person who repairs shoes). This was a common trade for deaf people when William was growing up.

But William never forgot his dream. He loved to play baseball. He had a great passion for it that matched his exceptional playing ability. He did not give up his dream, but he accepted his limitations. He worked very hard at school to learn the craft of shoemaking to please his parents. However, when he was not in class, he spent most of his free time practicing baseball skills, especially throwing.

William's father did not want William to play organized baseball. His father thought baseball players of that time generally did not display good character. Yet, William continued to play and practiced hard at school and at home to learn the game of baseball and to sharpen his skills.

William had a close friend named Ed Dundon, who was quite a good baseball player despite being deaf. William was very determined to succeed, even though almost everyone else thought he wouldn't. So, he decided to ask Ed to teach him some skills. Ed was very supportive and willing to help his deaf pal. Ed not only taught William baseball skills, but he also had some wise advice for William: "Just be better than anyone else." William carried those words with him for the rest of his life. He practiced long hours, worked hard, and developed a good character. Over time, William achieved remarkable success both on and off the playing field.

He was also blessed with natural talent and athletic skills. After years of practice and playing local street baseball games, William's skills impressed his coaches and his teammates. Several years after graduation, he opened a shoe repair store (cobbler's shop) in his hometown and worked hard at his craft. He played baseball on weekends, and eventually professional scouts from the big leagues noticed his skills. In 1886, seven years after graduating from the Ohio School for the Deaf, William began his professional career in Osh-kosh, Wisconsin. He had worked hard to overcome many obstacles and prejudices to reach that goal.

William was twenty-four years old when he realized his dream of playing professional baseball. Two years later, on April 20, 1888, he played his first game in the Major Leagues, with the Washington Senators. Now imagine you're William "Dummy" Hoy. It's your first time at bat in the majors. You're so excited, but you can't hear the umpire call a strike. You can't hear the last minute plays ordered by your coach. You can't even hear the cheers of the crowd...Because you're deaf.

Being deaf is a major challenge in life. It requires much work to overcome, but William Hoy is a good example of a deaf person who did succeed. He did overcome the challenges. By the end of his professional career, he was considered one of the most accomplished and most intelligent players in baseball. It's incredible that a deaf person could accomplish so much as a professional athlete. In his fourteen years in the Major Leagues, he had racked up league-leading hits, runs, and steals. He had become a baseball star and role model cheered by many fans across the country. By any standard,

The Story of William "Dummy" Hoy

William racked up some amazing statistics. *Baseball-reference. com* records the following:

- 2,048 total hits (another report states 2,054)
- 1,429 total runs scored
- 725 RBIs (runs batted in)
- .288 lifetime batting average
- .386 on-base percentage
- 40 home runs
- 1,006 walks
- 596 total stolen bases
- 3,964 career putouts (catching the ball in the outfield)

Chapter Two Questions

1. What caused William's deafness?

   _____

2. What was William's nickname and how did he get this nickname?

   _____

3. Who taught William baseball skills and gave him sound advice when he was a boy?

   _____

4. What was William's dream?

   _____

5. How old was William when he achieved his dream?

   _____

Fielding was quite a challenge without a glove.

Chapter Three
HAND SIGNALS

William began his professional career in 1886. Back then, the umpires just shouted out the calls to the players and spectators. William, of course, couldn't hear the umpires shout "strike" or "ball." That certainly put him at a big disadvantage. When he was at bat, he always had to turn and face the umpire to read his lips or use gestures to find out whether a ball or a strike had been called. Often, the pitcher on the opposing team would take advantage of William. He would pitch before William had turned around and was really ready to bat. So, William's batting average was a mere .219 for that first year. If he played like that today, he would certainly be cut from the team. But William's poor performance had nothing to do with his batting skills.

Instead of complaining or blaming his low batting average on his deafness or the other teams' tactics against him, William figured out a creative way to solve the problem. In his second year of professional play, William, a left-handed hitter, wrote a note to the third base coach. (See Figure 1 for the locations of the coaches' boxes, which were called captains' boxes in William's day). William asked the third base coach to motion with his left hand to signal a ball and his right hand for a strike. He based his simple instructions on the sign language he had learned when he studied at the Ohio School for the Deaf.

These simple hand movements made a major difference for him. Now, he could quickly "read" the hand signals after each pitch and be ready for the next pitch. Borrowing from American Sign Language, William also adapted signals for "out" and "safe." With the use of these hand signals, William's batting average soared to .367 for his second year of professional play. This was a .148 increase over the previous year! He now knew whether the umpire had called a strike or a ball and knew the pitch count (balls and strikes), and that the pitchers could no longer quick-pitch him. His skills came shining through. He helped his team win the Northwestern Pennant with both his remarkable batting and his fearless play in the outfield.

Before long, the third base coach began signaling the opposing team's balls and strikes to William as he played outfield. William then wrote a note, requesting the umpires to use hand signals. The umpires agreed with his request, and it wasn't too long before most of the umpires on the field used hand signals during William's games. The umpires continued to develop and use the hand signals throughout William's career and his Major League stats soared as a result. It is widely believed that the hand signals quickly became popular and served as the basis for the complex hand signals used by players, coaches, and umpires in every baseball game played for more than 100 years! They became standard practice. Signs used to steal a base, for pick-off plays, and for hit and run all likely evolved from William's creative use of hand signs. Players and fans today still benefit from the hand signals that William pioneered. (See Figure 2 for a chart of the more frequently used baseball signals utilized by umpires today.)

Figure 1

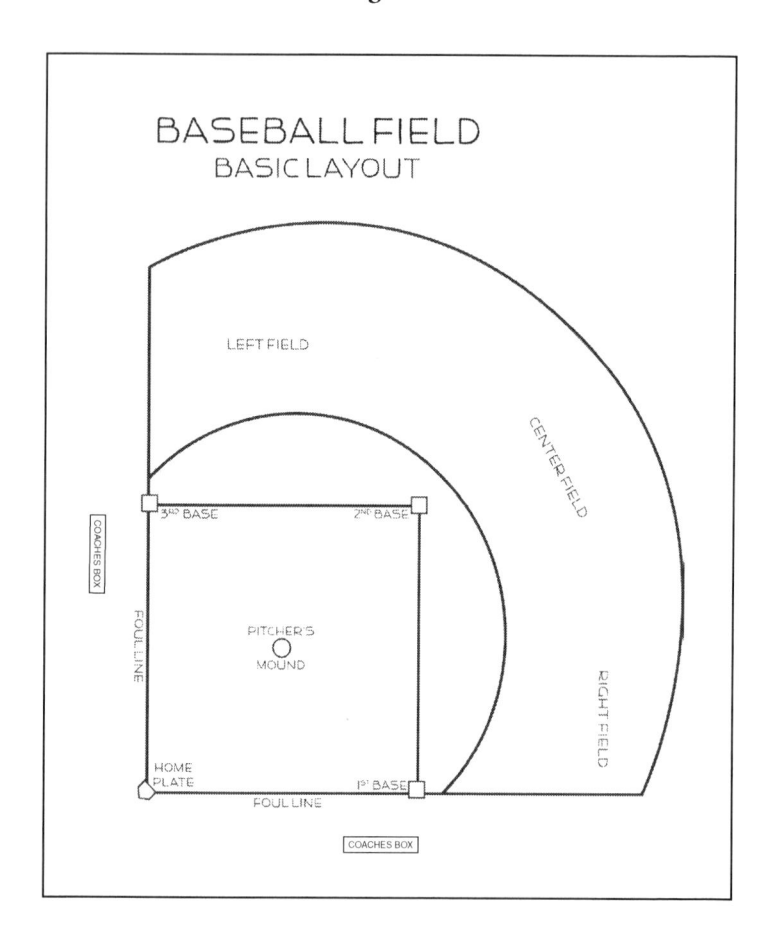

Figure 2

Baseball Signal Chart

A. Do Not Pitch
B. Play Ball
C. Time-Out, Foul Ball or Dead Ball
D. Delayed Dead Ball
E. Strike or Out
F. Infield Fly
G. Safe
H. Fair Ball
I. Foul Tip
J. Count
K. Time Play

Many people feel the current system of baseball hand signals can be traced back to William Hoy. Newspaper clippings from 1888 contain direct references to William and his use of hand signals. Other early deaf players, Edward Joseph "Dummy" Dundon and Luther Haden "Dummy" Taylor, also likely contributed to the use of these hand signals.

The Baseball Hall of Fame in Cooperstown, New York, however, credits the invention of hand signals to umpire Bill Klem in 1905. This was just two years after William retired from professional baseball. Mr. Klem was a very flamboyant umpire. He may well have improved and standardized the use of hand signals or added additional hand signals, but reports indicate that William and his coaches used hand signals in 1887. Charles Carraway in an 1888 report issued by the National Deaf-Mute College (now Gallaudet College) wrote: "When he (Hoy) bats, a man stands in the captain's box near third base and signals to him decisions of the umpire on balls and strikes by raising his fingers." (Silent World. PA School for the Deaf).

William didn't just rely on the hand signals he created. He also taught his teammates how to communicate in sign language. This proved to be very valuable on the field on certain occasions.

All the fans loved and respected William and his remarkable talent. They were quite inspired by the hand signals they saw on the playing field. Whenever he made an amazing play, thousands of fans would stand up in the bleachers and wave their arms and hats wildly to show their approval with "Deaf Applause." At those times of triumph, William could actually *see the crowd roar*.

William's story has inspired many people who have worked hard to achieve their dreams. He achieved his dream even though he was deaf. He learned how to cope with his deafness by developing signals, reading lips, and using sign language.

Joshua Leland Evans wrote it best in his article for *Sports Collectors Digest* (July 26, 1991):

> *Maybe William Hoy didn't hit as many home runs as Babe Ruth or Hank Aaron or have as many singles as Ty Cobb or Pete Rose. But he did more. He is a symbol of people who just need to be given a chance—a chance to be treated just like everyone else.*

Chapter Three Questions

1. What was William's disadvantage when he was batting?

2. How did he overcome this disadvantage?

3. How does an umpire signal a strike or an out (same signal for both)?

4. What is the umpire's signal that a base runner is safe?

5. Why did William's batting average drop to .219 his first year with Oshkosh?

6. What did William write on the note that he gave to the umpires?

7. What did the fans do whenever William made an outstanding play?

8. What was William's batting average his second year, when coaches and umpires used hand signals for him the entire year?

William's throwing record has stood the test of time.

Chapter Four

IT TAKES CHARACTER

Have you ever been bullied? Have you ever had someone make fun of you and call you names, because of the way you look, the way you dress, or what you do? It's not fun, is it?

It takes character to become a true winner like William "Dummy" Hoy. Becoming a person of character is an important part of following the "Golden Rule." *The Golden Rule says that you should treat people the way you would like other people to treat you.* Following the "Golden Rule" will help you attain excellence and achieve your goals.

It's simple. If you wouldn't like someone doing or saying something to you, you shouldn't do it or say it to someone else. Just imagine yourself in the exact place of the other person, in the same situation. Keep in mind what they like and dislike, and the situation they are in. If you ignore their point of view and act out anyway, then you're breaking the rule.

And if you pick on or make fun of another person, you are a bully. A good citizen is *not* a bully. Organized sports, such as baseball, are a great place to learn how to build good character and follow the "Golden Rule." Players, parents, and fans should always act with kindness and respect rather than bullying others. Yelling at someone or being hurtful to other people is a total rule breaker. When an opposing player makes a good play, you and your teammates should show good sportsmanship and compliment that player. You should not physically or verbally abuse someone who makes an error. That's bullying. It's far better to play in the spirit of respect and fairness, beginning with a positive "can do and will do" attitude that builds integrity—just as William did.

A person of character, like William Hoy:

- Has a positive attitude and is a productive person in society.
- Demonstrates qualities such as honesty and respect, good citizenship, teamwork, courage, and loyalty.
- Works hard to become the best person he/she can be.
- Develops his or her talents and skills through practice.
- Has high values, sets and reaches goals, and helps others, thereby achieving satisfaction and self-worth.

William was a young deaf boy who overcame great challenges to become a beloved, top-ranked Major League baseball star. His good character is shown clearly by the way he practiced, played, and lived his life. Therefore, William "Dummy" Hoy is an excellent example of a "CHARACTERED" person.

CHARACTERED is used here as an acronym. An acronym is formed from the first letter of a series of words. The acronym CHARACTERED is formed from words which are traits of good citizens. These traits describe values or virtues that can help you become a positive and productive person in life. This acronym will remind you how to behave as a person of character, like William, and how to treat your teammates, family, friends—and even foes—with kindness and respect.

Follow the CHARACTERED guidelines outlined in the acronym on the following page and you will always play and act like a champion—on and off the field.

A CHARACTERED© person exhibits these traits:

Courage............ by always doing what is needed and right, even in difficult situations

Honesty............ by always telling the truth

Accountablility.... by measuring results achieved versus goals and values

Respectfulness .... by always demonstrating and expecting courteous regard for others' feelings

Authenticity........ by remaining true to yourself and using your talents wisely

Commitment....... by always carrying through and doing what you say you will do

Trustworthiness .. by being dependble and reliable and believing in yourself

Ethical Behavior .. by doing what is morally right, which is often above and beyond what is acceptable legal behavior

Responsiblility .... by accepting the consequences of your actions from positive life lessons

Enlightenment .... by continually observing and learning from positive life lessons

Disciplined Behavior...by acting and reacting in a controlled and positive manner

Values are guiding principles that help people recognize right from wrong. A virtue is a positive, good characteristic that is highly valued. In simple terms, a virtue is a good and moral trait. Virtues lead you towards your own personal goals and society's goals. Success follows.

Character can be described as a set of behavior traits that defines what sort of person you are. For instance, a good behavior trait would be always respecting the calls of the umpire. A bad behavior trait would be repeatedly trying to shove a base runner off first base. CHARACTERED behavior determines how you will achieve goals in life, how you will deal with other people in society, and how you will obey the laws and rules of the group.

Organized sports, such as Little League Baseball, are a great place for young people to learn and develop good character. Becoming a "CHARACTERED" individual is a part of following the "Golden Rule." This is why the Little League mission states in part: "The Little League programs assist in developing the qualities of citizenship, discipline, teamwork, and physical well-being. By espousing the virtues of character, courage, and loyalty, The Little League Baseball and Softball Program is designed to develop superior citizens rather than superior athletes."

Developing good character leads to achieving goals and excellence.

Chapter Four Questions

1. What is the "Golden Rule?"

   _____

2. What is a virtue?

   _____

3. What is an acronym?

   _____

4. Becoming a "CHARACTERED" individual will help you become a true

   _____

5. Name at least three qualities of William Hoy that show that he was a "CHARACTERED" person.

   _____

Chapter Five
A COBBLER'S LIFE

Have you ever heard of the word *integrity*? Do you know what it means? Integrity is the quality of being honest and fair. Integrity is doing what is right, even when no one is watching and even though it may not benefit you. Integrity was one of the great characteristics that William Hoy possessed.

William was widely regarded as a "gentleman" on the field. Although teams clashed and fights broke out regularly back in those wild days of professional baseball, William never got thrown out of a game by an umpire for unsportsmanlike conduct.

Once, when the umpire asked if he had caught a ball legally (on the fly and not on a bounce), he answered honestly that he had not, and the umpire called the batter safe. Even in the face of his teammates' unhappy reaction to his honest answer to the umpire, William refused to back down and lie about the catch. The owner met William at the end of the game. He congratulated William and indicated that he'd rather lose a game than win by cheating. At the end of the season, the whole town of Oshkosh honored William as a star baseball player who played with the kind of honorable integrity they could admire.

William always played with honor and good character and felt confident that he had done the right thing. You, also, want to play with honor and do the right thing.

* * * * *

You might wonder why William became a cobbler. William spent his school years at the Ohio School for the Deaf. During that time, he was trained as a cobbler and learned how to repair shoes. Being a cobbler was one of the most common jobs for a deaf person in the 1800s. His well-meaning teachers at school and even his loving parents believed he had limited options in life. In their world, the idea of William becoming a professional baseball player was as likely as a man walking on the moon. As he once said, "Being handicapped by deafness, it was my thought I would make better progress in life if I worked as a cobbler and lived at home. My father told my brothers not to mislead me."

When William's brothers graduated from high school, their father gave them each a buggy, a harness, a saddle, and a new suit. William graduated from the Ohio School for the Deaf in 1879, at age seventeen, as the valedictorian of his class. He received a new suit and a promise that he could live rent-free in the family home until he was twenty-four. His parents simply assumed that William wouldn't be able to make it on his own without their help. In fact, most deaf people in William's time didn't have many opportunities other than a low-level job such as a cobbler.

Many people looked down on those who were deaf, because

they couldn't understand them. Employees applying for a job who could hear and speak almost always got the job, even if the deaf person had performed better.

So after graduation, William helped his dad on the family farm. But he was determined to be independent and useful in society. Therefore, he went to work at Mr. Beagle's cobbler shop. When he was twenty-two years old, he opened up his own repair shop, using the trade he had learned at school. At first, many people did not want a deaf person repairing their shoes. But William worked hard and did a very good job. Over time, the people liked William's work and only wanted to have him repair their shoes and boots. Before long, his shoe repair business was a success. He felt very blessed to have a steady income and a trade in spite of his hearing and speaking challenges.

William always intended to be an independent and responsible citizen. He also worked hard to break down the barrier between those who could hear and those who were deaf. He wanted to prove that people who could *not* hear nor speak *still* had qualities such as perseverance, patience, honesty, and respect.

One day, William noticed a boy with worn-out shoes, playing in the street. Taking the boy aside, William kindly looked over the raggedy shoes. Realizing there was no hope to repair them, William gave the boy a pair of shoes that he had repaired while learning his trade. That was the kind of generous person William was. He was following the "Golden Rule" and demonstrating his good character.

While he was quite busy and enjoying some success repairing shoes, William still dreamed of playing baseball. He refused to give up his dream of playing on a professional team. Most people in the rural areas where William lived were very poor. During the hot summer months, many people went barefoot. This caused business to slow down in William's shoe repair shop. William took advantage of these slow periods to practice his athletic skills, including playing ball in the street in front of his shop with the neighborhood kids. On weekends, he played baseball games with local amateur teams.

One day, a baseball scout (someone who looks for very good players) saw William playing in a street game. The scout was impressed by the little man's remarkable ability to throw a ball with such speed and accuracy. The scout tried to compliment William on his skills. The scout was very surprised to learn that this talented player was deaf and could not speak. At first, the scout decided to pass on William. However, the next day, the scout came back to the shop and invited William to play with a Kenton, Ohio team. The game was against a bitter rival team from Urbana. During the game, William easily got several hits off Billy Hart, the Urbana pitcher who was actually a professional player.

The scout was very impressed by William's baseball skills. He told William that he thought he could get a professional team to hire him. The very next day, William decided that he was ready to follow his dream to become a professional player. William knew his father didn't want him to play professional baseball, so he apologized to his father for going to Urbana to play. (And his father accepted his apology.) But William was so determined to pursue his Major League baseball career that he impulsively closed up his cobbler shop! He left the safety of its steady income behind. And soon, with the help of the scout, William was hired to join the Oshkosh Minor League team of the Northwestern League. This was the first time William played professional baseball.

A professional is a person engaged in an activity for pay. William was thrilled and grateful to the club management for giving him the chance to play for money. He had already spent much of his life proving that he could overcome the disadvantages of his hearing impairment on and off the field. William learned to ignore the insults and negative attitudes from so-called "normal" people. He continued to rely on the qualities of his good character, to believe in himself, and to live by his strong work ethic.

When William finished playing his first game with the Oshkosh club, he was so thrilled to be playing as a professional player that he didn't even take off his uniform in the locker room. He just sat down and wrote to his parents to share his exciting news! In spite of all the people who hadn't believed in him, William's dream of playing professional baseball was happening at last!

Although meningitis had changed his life forever at age three, William rejected the excuse that his deafness and his small size would prevent him from achieving his goal. He kept on working and improving his game, and his persistence rewarded him with what he wanted most—becoming a professional baseball player.

William always played by the rules—honoring and respecting both the game and his fellow players. Throughout his life on and off the field, cheating was something he would never do. Despite his own obvious disadvantages when playing baseball, William didn't believe he should ever try to win by cutting corners or cheating others and taking the glory. William wanted to break records, win games, and be the best asset he could be on his own merits. William believed that telling the truth and playing with honor was more important than winning a game.

William proved himself right. More importantly, he taught us all great lessons on how to become successful in life despite challenges and limitations.

Chapter Five Questions

1. What did William's father give him when he graduated from high school?

   _____

2. What was William's first job after graduation?

   _____

3. William signed his first *professional* contract with which team in which league?

   _____

4. What did William do during most of his spare time?

   _____

5. After his first professional game, what did William do before taking off his uniform?

   _____

Chapter Six
THE ROAD TO SUCCESS

Have you ever wanted to learn something or to do something so badly that you couldn't sleep and thought you might go crazy? You plaster your wall with pictures, you think and dream about it all day long and all night, and yet… You fear that you might fail. What you need is the courage to step bravely forward and follow your dream.

William summoned up that courage on the day that he locked up his cobbler shop and set out on the road to find a team that would hire him. He believed in himself and his ability to play baseball, and he believed in the scout who told him that he could find a professional team that would hire him. He was willing to sacrifice his income as a cobbler to pursue his dream.

Applying for a position on a baseball team can be very intimidating for anyone, no matter how good the person is. You have to steel your nerves, use all your courage, and focus on the "task at hand." Can you imagine the courage it took for a young, small, deaf cobbler to present himself to the powerful managers and owners of professional baseball teams?

One of the scout's first attempts to get William a position on a professional team was with the Milwaukee Brewers, a Major League team. The team was interested because of William's skills. However, the manager was very disrespectful. When he learned that William was deaf and unable to speak, he even laughed at William for wanting to play on his team. The manager didn't take William seriously, and the club made William a very poor offer that didn't match his obvious abilities. William didn't accept the offer. Despite his dreams, William ended the meeting by writing a note to the manager and owner informing them that he would not play for their team, even for a million dollars. That was a huge amount of money in the late 1880s. It required courage and *self-respect* to turn down this opportunity to play professional baseball.

But William was persistent, as well as courageous. He wouldn't give up. In another attempt to play for a different team, William wrote on a piece of paper: "Give me a chance. Give me an opportunity." He even offered to try out for free just to show the manager that he could play. William promised the manager that if he didn't agree that he could play, he would leave. He proved that he was a good hitter and a speedy defensive player with a powerful and accurate arm. He won over the skeptical manager, Frank Selee, of the Osh-kosh (Wisconsin) team.

It also took courage on the part of Frank Selee to hire a player who could neither hear nor speak. But Frank Selee was noted for his ability to assess and utilize talent, and he recognized the talent of young William. William was fortunate to be hired by Frank Selee, because he was an adept handler of players. He knew how to utilize their talents. He became a very successful manager who was elected to the Baseball Hall of Fame in 1999. William had two great years with Oshkosh and Frank Selee.

After those two successful years playing on a minor league team, the Major League Milwaukee Brewers contacted William to play for their team. They were impressed with his .367 batting average the previous season as well as his speed and defense in centerfield. However, William remembered the lack of respect he had received when he had negotiated with the club before. He didn't want to play for a manager who had shown him such disrespect, even if it meant losing out on an opportunity with a Major League club. So, William rejected their offer…a second time! After that, William became widely respected for his integrity and character.

Sometimes, you have to wait for the right opportunity. That, too, can take courage. This time, William didn't have to wait long for the Washington Senators to grab him, and he was on the way to a successful, fourteen-year career in the Major Leagues.

William's hard work, determination, and courage proved his critics wrong and helped his dreams come true. He was doing what he did best—playing baseball. It could have made William proud and conceited, but instead he was humbled by this show of acceptance and respect by the fans.

Whenever William made an outstanding play, they didn't cheer loudly. Instead, the crowd in the stands would stand and wildly wave their arms and their hats to show William their approval. Think of it as an early version of the "wave" fans do at stadiums during today's games. This sea of approval must have thrilled William as he looked up at the soundless sight. Whenever he *saw* the crowd roar, William was thankful for the opportunity he had been given to prove that he could not only overcome his handicaps, but also become one of the best in the game. He had, indeed, beaten the odds!

Later in his life, William was asked what it took for him to succeed as a deaf ball player in the Major Leagues. His sign language reply was: "It is not enough that the deaf candidate for baseball honors has the necessary ability, he assuredly must have the nerve and the courage to even apply for a trial."

Chapter Six Questions

1. What was the name of the first team to offer William a contract?

   _____

2. Why did William not accept this contract?

   _____

3. How many years did William play in the minors before being hired by a Major League team?

   _____

4. What did William do best?

   _____

William had a .288 lifetime batting average.

Chapter Seven
THE WONDER YEARS

Have you ever worked very hard for something and then had it pay off? Do you remember the happy feeling you had inside? Hard work, honest effort, and dedication to something you love definitely can pay off. William Hoy experienced that satisfaction when he played his first professional game for the Oshkosh team in 1886 and achieved his dream. That feeling is one of the greatest rewards of setting and reaching almost any goal in life.

William's success was a surprise to many people who had thought the odds were stacked so high against him. But it was no surprise to him with his never-give-up attitude. It had simply been his goal, and he'd worked hard to get there, always believing in himself.

William loved to play baseball. He played a total of eighteen seasons with professional teams (fourteen with Major League teams). He secured his place on the leader boards in the majors by racking up league-leading hits, runs, and steals. And he recorded some tremendous plays in the minors, too.

William had a great season with the Minor League Oshkosh team in 1887. He then moved up to the Major Leagues and played for the Washington Senators in 1888.

When the new deaf rookie arrived at the Washington Senators ball club, he immediately posted a statement on the clubhouse wall. Since he could neither hear nor speak, he explained how he called for a ball by squeaking loudly. If they didn't hear him squeak loudly, then he wasn't going after the ball. He wanted this understood to avoid collisions with the other fielders.

William clearly understood that communication was extremely important in baseball. He always tried to make it easier on the hearing people around him to accept and understand his disability and work together as a team. He was considered to be very polite and was well liked by his teammates. There's no record of William ever being thrown out of a game for misconduct. This is a very remarkable feat. In those days, baseball was a rough-and-tumble sport; unfortunately, fights frequently occurred.

In his rookie year in the Major Leagues, William continued to use his speed and quick thinking to his advantage. William was an exceptional base stealer, leading the league with eighty-two stolen bases his rookie year. But that kind of success gave the surprise rookie star some new challenges the following season. The pitchers and catchers of the rival teams had heard about this amazing base stealer. They focused more of their attention on William as a result. But they still couldn't stop him. In 1889, he still scored ninety-eight runs and stole thirty-three bases, with an on-base percentage of .376.

During his rookie year, William also had sixty-nine walks, the second highest in his league. Since he was only 5'4" tall and weighed about 148 pounds, he had a small strike zone. With a great eye for the ball, he used his short stature to his advantage. By the time he retired in 1902, William placed second in Major League history with more than 1,006 career walks. This statistic shows that he was a team player, willing to sacrifice the opportunity for a hit just to get on base and help his team.

Although he was a small man, William demonstrated admirable athletic abilities in speed, dexterity, and throwing accuracy. His overall defensive skills were impressive. William was the first outfielder to play centerfield very shallow. He was able to come in quickly for a weakly hit ball. With his speed, he could also turn and get to balls hit deep into the outfield. This strategy, along with his speed and a strong throwing arm, set the standard for future center fielders. This was another of William's contributions to the game of baseball.

According to an article by Ralph Berger for the Society for American Baseball Research, "Hoy is one of three outfielders to throw out three base runners at home plate in one game. On June 19, 1889, he 'fired' perfect strikes to catcher Connie Mack to throw out runners attempting to score from second base." It's a record that has been tied twice, but never broken. Some writers have referred to William's throwing arm as a "cannon," meaning it was super strong and accurate.

Tommy Leach, who was William's roommate in 1899, described what it was like to play in a game with William:

> We got to be good friends. He was a real fine ballplayer. When you played with him in the outfield, the thing was that you never called for a ball. You listened for him, and if he made this little squeaky sound, that meant he was going to take it....We hardly ever had to use our fingers to talk, though most of the fellows did learn the sign language, so that when we got confused or something, we could straighten it out with our hands.

William and his teammates occasionally did have communication problems. Once, his team was scheduled to play an exhibition game in Paterson, New Jersey. However, the manager failed to notify William in sign language or in writing of the early morning departure. When the team met in the hotel lobby to take the train, William was not there. Some players went up to his room. They began to yell and knock loudly to get him to wake up. Of course, none of that worked. The noise literally fell on William's deaf ears. One of the smaller men attempted to squeeze through the window above the door. Then, they tried to squeeze a young bellboy through the overhead window, but even he was too big to get through. The players threw several plugs of tobacco at William, hitting him in the shoulder. They even tossed a deck of cards for the cause, and the cards landed in a colorful spread all over William. Still, the players got no response. Finally, someone tied a set of keys to a sheet and tossed it through the window. They managed to drag the keys across William until one snagged on his shirt.

Finally, William woke up in a fog to find a mess of playing cards, wads of tobacco, and other objects spread all over him. He assumed his teammates had been playing a prank on him. He immediately grabbed a pitcher of water and threw it right at the faces that appeared in the window above his door. Once everything was explained, and apologies were offered and accepted, even William got a good laugh over that comedy of errors. After that, he always made sure the front office informed him of any changes in the schedule.

William played for the Chicago White Stockings of the new American League in 1900. However, the American League did not officially become a Major League until 1901, so William's statistics from 1900 are not officially included as part of his Major League career. Yet, according to baseball historian Nicholas Dawidoff, William recorded defensive statistics that season that have never been duplicated in professional baseball. He led the league with 337 putouts, a .977 fielding percentage and 45 assists, while playing just 137 games. Dawidoff wrote: "It was the only time an outfielder has ever led the majors in all three defensive categories!" One could call these the "Triple Crown" of defense.

As a league leader in assists, William had such a powerful throwing arm that he could throw strike after strike to home plate from centerfield. Because of this ability, along with his impressive speed and fast thinking on the field, William was one of the great "flyhawks" (fast, skilled outfielders) of the era.

He was well regarded for his honesty, respect for his fellow teammates, knowledge of the game, and sense of fair play. William also made a name for himself as one of the original "spark-plugs" (team leader or captain).

William was involved in a unique situation in 1902: two deaf players faced off against each other in a Major League game. It was pitcher Luther "Dummy" Taylor of the New York Giants versus batter William "Dummy" Hoy of the Cincinnati Reds. The two deaf players "spoke" to each other briefly through sign language. On William's first time at bat, he greeted Taylor by hand signing, "I'm glad to see you!" Then he promptly drove a single to center. Dr. Lawrence Fleischer, a leader in the deaf community, once commented on that historic event that has never been repeated since that banner day:

> *That particular meeting has always inspired me, because it was deaf versus deaf in that particular game, and it's a very rare moment...Today many deaf children do know who William Hoy is, as well as Dummy Taylor. They are role models for many of today's children. I would hope to see something like that happen again in the future.*

To his credit, William overcame the disadvantages and struggles of a deaf person in a hearing world. He excelled, because he believed in himself. He always gave 100 percent effort, even down to his very last game.

In 1903, his last year of professional baseball, William

played for the Los Angeles LooLoos of the Pacific Coast League. He was an "old man" of 41, yet he played in all 211 games on the schedule that year. William finally retired at the end of the season—but not before scoring 156 runs, stealing 46 bases, recording 419 putouts, and leading his team to a remarkable year-ending game and season.

William's final play as a professional baseball player is perhaps the most amazing play ever in professional baseball. It was the ninth inning. The opposing team had base runners. Los Angeles was ahead by only one run. The batter of the opposing team drove the fly ball deep into center field. Everyone thought it would be a game-winning home run. William squeaked loudly to alert the other outfielders that he planned to catch the ball. He made a beeline towards the line of fans spread out very deep in center field. He was determined to catch the ball and prevent a home run. Running at full speed, William leaped on a horse's back that was blocking his path to the ball. Using the horse as a springboard, he leaped again to make a stunning catch that saved the game and won the pennant for his team. Once again, William was a hero to his team and his fans. His amazing play actually made *headlines* in the newspaper. To his very last play, William knew how to make his presence known in a very positive way!

Chapter Seven Questions

1. When William arrived at the Washington Senators ball club, what did the rookie do immediately?

2. What record does William hold that has been tied twice but never broken?

3. What is the nickname given to a skilled, speedy outfielder?

4. What was the nickname given to team captains in William's time?

5. Name the last professional team William played on.

6. What role did a horse play in William's final play of his career?

William Hoy was inducted into the Cincinnati Reds Hall of Fame in 2003.

Anna Maria Hoy,
William's beloved wife.

Chapter Eight

IT'S A WONDERFUL LIFE AFTER MAJOR LEAGUE BASEBALL

A true baseball hero not only scores many runs, breaks records, and wins games, but he also displays character and winning behavior on and off the field. Being a good sport goes well beyond the playing field. Even after retiring from baseball, William Hoy continued being a "CHARACTERED" person throughout his life.

After his Major League career was established, William "Dummy" Hoy married his sweetheart, Anna Maria Lowry, on October 26, 1898. They unselfishly promised to love, honor, and respect each other for the rest of their lives. Anna Maria was also deaf. She became a prominent teacher of the deaf at the same Columbus school where William had studied.

William was on the road, focusing on baseball during the season. He was, however, a devoted family man. He and

Anna Maria raised their hearing children to be responsible, hardworking, and caring members of the community. Their son, Carson, became a lawyer and judge. Daughters Carmen and Clover became schoolteachers. He was very proud of his children. He once walked an amazing seventy-two blocks at the age of eighty to see his son, Judge Carson Hoy, preside in court.

William's generous character was clearly evident when he gladly accepted the responsibility of raising his nephew, Paul Helms. Paul was the son of William's sister, Ora, who had died when Paul was only three years old. Paul's father was quite ill and sent young Paul to live with his uncle. With the financial support and love of William and his new family, Paul went on to earn a degree from Syracuse University. He later established Helms Bakery and financed the U.S. Olympic Committee in 1932 and 1936. With Helms Bakery, Paul became a millionaire. With his new fortune, he founded and sponsored the Helms Athletic Foundation and Helms Hall in Los Angeles.

As a man of great character and intelligence, William enjoyed financial and personal success in his later years. After he retired from baseball, William purchased a farm in Mount Healthy, Ohio, and became a successful dairy farmer. To help with the war effort, he supervised hundreds of deaf workers at the Goodyear Tire Company. After his children left home, William sold the farm and worked at a book company until he finally retired at the age of seventy-five!

William's joy of life was dampened when his dear wife, Anna Maria, died at age seventy-five. The pains of this loss were deep. However, his natural courage and enthusiasm for life helped him to recover from this painful loss. Age did not slow him down. He still danced the Charleston and pruned fruit trees in his eighties.

✳ ✳ ✳ ✳ ✳

William maintained his love for baseball after his final professional season in 1903. He never chased the limelight and never looked for glory for himself. After his baseball career was over, he used his celebrity status to foster the needs and concerns of the deaf. He was active in the deaf community as well as in youth and adult baseball and softball organizations. He continued to be involved in the sport by coaching and playing on deaf teams. He actually harbored another dream that lasted until the end of his life: he wanted an all-mute baseball team. Responding to an interview about a baseball team made up of only deaf players, William wrote:

> *While this dream of an all-mute baseball team will hardly come true in the immediate future, there is room, nevertheless, for a mute or two in the big leagues now. It only remains for them to come boldly forward and make a try.*

In recognition of his remarkable career in Major League Baseball, William was given a silver pass from both the American and National League presidents. These passes allowed him to attend any Major League game without paying. He used both passes often, but he did not attend crowded opening-day games. Although scorecards were not used in William's day, he likely would have enjoyed scoring some of these games. (See Appendix 2 for a sample scorecard and more information on scoring.)

William felt quite honored to be the first deaf athlete inducted into the American Athletic Association of the Deaf Hall of Fame. Today, there's even a baseball field named in his honor at the Gallaudet University School for the Deaf in Washington, DC.

On October 7, 1961, ninety-nine-year-old William was invited to throw out the ceremonial first pitch before game three of the World Series. William was the oldest living former

Major League baseball player at that time. The big game was between the Cincinnati Reds and the New York Yankees in his beloved hometown of Cincinnati, Ohio. He was hailed as a living legend, and the cheering fans waved wildly when he was introduced to throw out the first pitch.

On that last day at Crosley Field, William was a living witness to the old game of his time and the new game of the modern era. William really enjoyed that special day. For the final time, he could *see the crowd roar*. It was his last appearance on a baseball field.

William died about two months later on December 15, 1961, and was survived by two children, seven grandchildren, and eight great-grandchildren. Discipline and hard work had been the core of his life. He was a shining example of a loving father, a faithful husband, and a wonderful grandfather and great-grandfather.

William was widely respected by his family, his teammates, and his extended community far beyond the baseball diamond. His life was defined by his amazing baseball statistics, his public honors and accomplishments, and his deep love for his family. Far from being just an ordinary man, William was indeed extraordinary.

Chapter Eight Questions

1. Whom did William marry on October 26, 1898?

2. What did William do to support his family when he first retired from baseball?

3. What other job did he take during World War I?

4. What did William do after he retired from the business world?

5. At the age of 80, how many blocks did William walk to see his son, Judge Carson Hoy, preside in court?

6. What did William do at age ninety-nine before game three of the World Series between the Cincinnati Reds and the New York Yankees?

7. What was another of William's dreams besides playing professional baseball?

William's batting average soared after he set up signals.

Chapter Nine

THE GREAT AMERICAN PASTIME—
YESTERDAY AND TODAY

We have this idea that the game has always been the same, that it's written in stone, but the fact is, it's changed a whole lot.

—**Warren Goldstein, author of**
Playing for Keeps: A History of Early Baseball

In 1896, while playing with the Cincinnati Reds, William and a teammate tied for the team lead with a season total of four home runs each! This is an example of how different baseball was back in the nineteenth century. Today, almost all players have more than four home runs.

When William was playing in the Major Leagues back in the late 1800s, the world of baseball was far different from the way things are today. The uniforms, equipment, safety measures, and the attitudes of owners and players were just some of the differences. Uniforms were usually made of flannel (wool). Batters didn't wear helmets, and catchers didn't wear masks. These safety measures commonly used today were not standard features until the twentieth century. It was also easier to cheat on the field, because there were fewer umpires working the game.

When William first started playing baseball, none of the players in the field used padded gloves. Some players were wearing regular leather work gloves that provided very little protection. William said he broke every finger at least once over the span of his career. This made it painful and difficult to even use sign language to communicate.

There were also no fences around many local ballparks; it was more like a community park. Fans would arrive by horse and buggy and set up a picnic. They would then watch the game from their comfortable perch, often deep in the outfield. This was much like the modern tailgate parties held in the parking lots of sports stadiums on game day.

In the late 1800s, there was certainly no loud speaker system wired throughout the stadium, no wireless microphone packs attached to the umpires, no play-by-play announcers perched high above the field in a skybox. And for sure, there were no convenient giant flat screens to watch the instant replays in HD.

The baseball game that William knew evolved from an amateur, club-based sport. William and his fellow teammates didn't make much money. In the late 1800s, most players, like William, played for the love of the game—not for the love of money.

The first all-professional team—the Cincinnati Red Stockings—was formed in 1869, just seven years after William was born. The highest paid player on that team was shortstop George Wright, who earned $1,400 per season. Calculated by today's standards, that equals just $23,000 a year. That's a long way from the millions earned by a single ball player today!

The average player on a professional team during the 1869 season earned about as much as a humble craftsman, such as a cobbler, did in a year. William's hard work and responsible determination to learn the trade of shoe repair at the same time that he was learning baseball came in handy. William, like many other players, needed to pick up other work in the off-season to support his family.

Today, the Great American Pastime has become a big business with huge salaries and elaborate baseball complexes. There are electronic scoreboards, fountains, and many fan amenities. Major League baseball clubs in 2014 have a lot of money to spend on their teams. According to celebritynetworth.com, when their salaries are combined, the top-tier baseball players are paid $364 million per year!

Today, when they're not playing, most professional baseball players invest time strengthening their bodies and getting in shape at a gym. In William's time, there were very few gyms. The game of baseball demands both physical and mental skills, yet baseball players in the 1800s were not considered very athletic by their fans. They weren't muscular the way many players on the current rosters are. Today's players can benefit from the wonders of medical science, and physical fitness and health programs help improve their performance.

Unfortunately, over the years, some athletes have chosen to misuse medical science, especially with the use of banned drugs. They are more interested in their personal success than the betterment of baseball and their team. The drive for money, power, and fame can damage a person's character and ultimately ruin his or her life. Honesty, fairness, and team spirit are sometimes thrown out the window in order to achieve higher personal statistics and pick up a larger paycheck.

The amazing careers and lifetime achievements of great players such as Barry Bonds, Roger Clemens, and Alex Rodriguez have been permanently tarnished by their admitted use of illegal or banned drugs. The baseball world was shocked and disappointed when their doping scandals were revealed.

Of course, baseball isn't the only sport to be caught in the issue of steroids and other banned substances. Champion athletes in the Olympics, NFL, NBA, and professional cycling have been caught cheating with steroids and other drugs. Some have been forced to return their medals in disgrace. Their careers, reputations, and lives have been damaged forever. Don't allow this to happen to you.

It takes a lot of character to resist taking the easy way to national fame or a big payday. It takes a lot of character and courage to resist using performance-enhancing drugs or gambling. This is why it's so important to concentrate on building and improving your character and baseball skills. It's not easy to "just say no." Unless you have a strong foundation of honesty, discipline, ethics, and trustworthiness, the temptation to do the wrong thing is hard to resist.

The great Pete Rose, "Mr. Hustle," is an example of how quickly an unwise choice can destroy one's character. In 1989, Pete Rose was the all-time Major League leader in hits (4,256), games played (3,562), at-bats (14,053), and outs (10,328). He had won three World Series championships, had three batting titles, a Most Valuable Player Award, two Gold Gloves, and the Rookie of the Year Award. Yet, in spite of all these awards, Pete Rose, the manager of the Cincinnati Reds, gambled on Reds games and was punished with a *lifetime ban* from baseball. And the entire world heard of his disgrace.

When William was playing in the Major Leagues, the newspaper sportswriters were basically the only sources for baseball news. Players were interviewed and quoted all the time. However, access to the players was mostly limited to the games and practices, personal interviews, and team outings. If a pitcher made a terrible pitch, or an outfielder dropped an easy fly ball, it might be in the local newspapers the next day. This might cause much embarrassment, but baseball fans beyond the local area never saw the local newspapers. Today, those same terrible pitches and dropped fly balls are captured on hundreds of smart-phones. Then they're posted on the Internet and go viral within hours. Soon fans across the entire US and even in foreign countries see them. What a difference from 125 years ago!

Unfortunately, behaving badly and displaying poor sportsmanship on the field have always been a part of the game, from William's time to the present day. Throwing a tantrum over the umpire's call, pitchers "accidentally" hitting batters, and bad reactions to being called "out" at the plate took place then, too. Unfortunately, there have always been a few, undisciplined players.

When a game, a pennant, or a championship is on the line, some players want to win so badly that good character and good sportsmanship go out the window. Sadly, that negative attitude can infect people on the sidelines or in the stands. This can be seen in the poor behavior and reactions of fans, parents, and even coaches at games, even in youth leagues. The need to win and be #1 at any cost can ruin the spirit of the game for everyone.

William lived and played in an era when some things were simpler, but everyday life was quite hard. From the beginning of his career, William didn't make much money and had to work as a cobbler in the off season. He had to put up with the prejudice of others because of his deafness, and most of all, he had to work harder than anyone else to prove himself every day. Yet, William strongly believed that as a deaf person, he had to always use tact and diplomacy—whether he was playing with his team, meeting with fans, or negotiating terms with his team.

William was a very private man, who was very polite and respectful to everyone. If there was any kind of misunderstanding, William was always very patient. He would keep trying to communicate until the other person finally realized his true meaning. It didn't matter whether the other person was deaf or could hear.

Today, medical and technical advances, TV, movies, books, and magazines promote the national fame and great financial rewards of baseball superstars. Today's superstars are admired by millions of fans. However, William Hoy still shines as a positive role model for all ages.

Chapter Nine Questions

1. What material were baseball players' uniforms made of back in the 1800s?

   _____

2. Why did William break every finger at least once?

   _____

3. Why was baseball superstar Pete Rose punished with a lifetime ban from baseball?

   _____

4. Who was the highest paid player on the Cincinnati Red Stockings in 1869 and how much did he earn?

   _____

5. What is the combined total of the top-tiered baseball players in 2014?

   _____

6. As a deaf person, what did William strongly believe?

   _____

Chapter Ten

THE GREAT DEBATE OF COOPERSTOWN

With his career achievements and contributions to baseball, why hasn't William "Dummy" Hoy been inducted into the National Baseball Hall of Fame? It's a question many of William's friends, family, and fans, along with baseball historians, have asked for decades. William himself reportedly said, "My two wishes in life are to live to be 100 years old and be in the Baseball Hall of Fame."

He nearly got his first wish when he lived to be 99 ½ years old, but he has yet to be elected to baseball's greatest honor roll. His granddaughter, Joan Sampson—who still lives in her family's hometown of Cincinnati—has said, "I'm sure my grandfather would love to be in Cooperstown. He was very proud of his career."

The National Baseball Hall of Fame and Museum is nicknamed Cooperstown, because it is located in Cooperstown, New York. It is a privately owned and operated museum that focuses on the study of the history of baseball. It also displays baseball-related artifacts and exhibits and honors the leaders and stars of the sport. The Hall of Fame's motto is: "Preserving History, Honoring Excellence, Connecting Generations."

The USA Deaf Sports Federation has lobbied since 1991 to get William into the Hall of Fame. More recently, the Hoy Committee has been campaigning for William's induction. They brought his case to the attention of the Veterans Committee of the Hall of Fame, which is responsible for nominating players from past eras. The committee's activities have increased William's visibility to the powers that be in Cooperstown.

William's name has been included on the ballots a number of times. William was close to making it in 1999, when Frank Selee was inducted into the Hall of Fame in the nineteenth century player category. You might recall that Frank managed the Oshkosh team where William got his start in professional baseball back in 1886.

In spite of the all these efforts, William has not yet been elected to the National Baseball Hall of Fame. Convinced that William is worthy of honor and recognition, his supporters wait until the next election and try again. William's supporters have established a website to gather signatures for a petition to secure a place in the Hall of Fame:

http://www.change.org/petitions/nominate-dummy-hoy-to-the-baseball-hall-of-fame

Even though he hasn't made the Hall of Fame, William has been recognized for excellence from some impressive sources. In 1939, he attended a Cincinnati Reds reunion. Former teammates Connie Mack and Clark Griffith were there, along with Sam Crawford and Honus Wagner. They all believed William deserved to be in the Hall of Fame. The four men campaigned for this honor to be given to their Cincinnati teammate. At this meeting, Sam Crawford, a member of the Hall of Fame, even said: "Did you know that he [William] was the one responsible for the umpire giving hand signals for a ball or strike? Raising his right hand for a strike, that's where the hand signals for the umpires calling balls and strikes began. That's a fact. Very few people know that." Baseball historian Greg Rhodes has noted: "They did not have all-star teams in Hoy's era, but if they did, he would have been on it every year."

Many other honors have been bestowed upon William Hoy. In 1941, William was inducted into the Louisville Colonels Hall of Fame. William has also been honored by the Cincinnati Reds (Reds Hall of Fame), the Ohio School for the Deaf, Ohio Baseball's "Stars in their Time," Hancock County Sports, and the Baseball Reliquary's Shrine of the Eternals. And in 1951, William was the first player to enter the American Athletic Association for the Deaf Hall of Fame.

William contributed to the history of the game. He excelled, as documented by a record that still stands nearly 125 years after he last played and by the following achievements. Additional information is included in Appendix 1, including a comparison with four other outfielders who have been elected the Hall of Fame.

William Hoy Career Highlights & Achievements

- In 1888, as a rookie, led the National League in stolen bases with 82—a record that stood for 97 years. Now second all-time for a rookie.

- One of the all-time leaders in stolen bases (Robert F. Panara ranked him 13th).

- Twice led the league in walks, and once in stolen bases and at-bats.

- Scored over 100 runs per season nine different times.

- On June 19, 1889, he threw perfect strikes from centerfield to catcher Connie Mack to throw out three different runners attempting to score from second base—a record that still stands today.

- Eighth all-time in double plays by an outfielder (retired as second).

- Fourteenth all-time in assists by an outfielder.

- Only professional outfielder to lead league in three primary defensive categories in one year: putouts, fielding average and assists—The "Triple Crown" of defense.

- At the time of his retirement, he was second in bases-on-balls ("walks") with 1,006.

- Mordecai Brown Player of the Decade (1890-1899).

- Most Inspirational Superstar of the 1890s.

- Fifth all-time best rookie season by a centerfielder (1888).

- National League Rookie of the Year in 1888 (retroactively).

- Played professional baseball from the age of 25 until the age of 42.

- His lifetime achievements, after playing in a record 1,797 games, ranked among some of the best in baseball.

- A very proficient left-handed batter and right-handed thrower, William played with four out of the five Major

Leagues in the country, which is an impressive feat on its own.

William Hoy's Professional Teams (1886-1903)

Pro Teams (but not Major League)

- Oshkosh—Northwestern League (1886-1887)
- Chicago White Stockings—American League (1900)
- Los Angeles LooLoos—Pacific League (1903)

Major League Teams

- Washington Senators—National League (1888-1889)
- Buffalo Bisons—Player's League (1890)
- St. Louis Browns—American Association (1891)
- Washington Senators—National League (1892-1893)
- Cincinnati Reds—National League (1894-1897)
- Louisville Colonels—National League (1898-1899)
- Chicago White Stockings—American League (1901)
- Cincinnati Reds—National League (1902)

William's integrity, sportsmanship, character, and other contributions to the sport of baseball should also be given considerable weight. After all, he pioneered the use of hand signals that have benefited players and fans for 125 years. He introduced the concept of playing a shallow centerfield. And who in baseball is a more inspiring role model to those with physical challenges than William Hoy?

As Leland Evans indicated in *Sports Collectors Digest* (July

26, 1991), William is a symbol for people who just need to be given a chance.

In the Hoy Committee's quest to elect William to The National Baseball Hall of Fame, they posted the following statement on the William Hoy petition website: "Mr. Hoy missed his first wish by dying at the age of 99, having thrown out the first ball in the third game of the 1961 World Series in Cincinnati. It is our fervent hope that he will get his final wish."

And so, the campaign continues to secure William's second wish: induction into the Baseball Hall of Fame.

Chapter Ten Questions

1. What were William's two wishes in life?
   _____

2. What is the National Baseball Hall of Fame and Museum in Cooperstown, New York?
   _____

3. What are the names of the two main organizations lobbying for William to be elected to the Hall of Fame?
   _____

4. Who was inducted into the Hall of Fame in 1999 in the 19th century player category?
   _____

5. In 1951, William was the first player to be entered into what Hall of Fame?
   _____

6. How many games did William play in during his professional career?
   _____

7. How many times did William score over 100 runs in one season?
   _____

8. Will you support the effort to get William Hoy elected to the National Baseball Hall of Fame? _____. If so, then visit the following website to add your name to the petition.

   http://www.change.org/petitions/nominate-dummy-hoy-to-the-baseball-hall-of-fame

HOY FIELD
William "Dummy" Hoy
1862 - 1961

Centerfielder
First Deaf Major League Baseball Pioneer
Invented Signs for "Strike" and "Ball"
Lifetime Batting .288
607 Stolen Bases
Threw Out 3 Men
At Home Plate In One Game

April 8, 2001

Conclusion

ADVERSITY CAN BE YOUR FRIEND

We've all heard the phrase: "Whatever doesn't kill you makes you stronger." In other words, adversity can actually be an advantage in disguise. Sometimes, what seems like a big disadvantage or hardship can actually turn out to be a benefit or an advantage.

A person may be forced to compensate for difficult conditions and to learn skills beyond the ones needed for a normal life. Being forced to cope with being deaf in a hearing world challenged William "Dummy" Hoy, too. But it also made him extra determined to find a way to follow his dream and the advice of his old friend, Ed Dundon: "Be better than anyone else." As he was growing up, William practiced long and hard to be the best that he could be. Thus, his speed, agility, and quick-thinking intelligence surprised his competitors, who expected him to fail.

Everyone loves the story of the underdog who beats the odds and comes out on top, just as William did. We root for the regular guy who manages to make something out of nothing by transforming himself or herself through hard work and positive thinking.

William fought hard to overcome the prejudices he encountered as a deaf person. It was especially difficult to be a deaf ballplayer. Even when people disrespected him, he was determined to show the world that he could be a quality Major League baseball player. He never made excuses for any problems encountered because he couldn't hear or speak. Instead, he pushed the limits of adversity and made adversity his friend.

William didn't give up. He put forth an impressive effort that led to a life of extraordinary achievement.

William was a CHARACTERED winner—on and off the field!

Are you a true winner? Are you CHARACTERED?

Appendix 1
William Hoy Statistics

ACTUAL MAJOR LEAGUE STATISTICS

PLAYER	Games	At Bats	Runs	Hits	RBI	Total Bases	BB	SO	AVE	Chances	Putouts	Double Plays
				OFFENSIVE							DEFENSIVE	
Brock, Lou	2616	10332	1610	3023	900	6713	761	1730	0.293	4732	4394	29
Carey, Max	2476	9363	1545	2665	800	5906	1040	695	0.285	6937	6363	87
Henderson, Ricky	3081	10961	2295	3055	1115	9057	2190	1694	0.279	6740	6468	23
Hoy, William	1797	7115	1429	2048	725	2658	1006	345	0.288	4632	3964	72
McCarthy, Tommy	1273	5120	1066	1493	732	3214	536	185	0.292	2544	2016	60

BASED ON SAME NUMBER OF GAMES & AT BATS

PLAYER	Games	At Bats	Runs	Hits	RBI	Total Bases	BB	SO	AVE	Chances	Putouts	Double Plays
				OFFENSIVE							DEFENSIVE	
Brock, Lou	1797	7115	1109	2082	620	4623	524	1191	0.293	3251	3018	20
Carey, Max	1797	7115	1174	2025	608	4488	750	528	0.285	5035	4618	63
Henderson, Ricky	1797	7115	1490	1983	724	5879	1422	1100	0.279	3931	3772	13
Hoy, William	1797	7115	1429	2048	725	2658	1006	345	.0288	4632	3964	72
McCarthy, Tommy	1797	7115	1481	2075	1017	4466	745	257	0.292	3591	2846	85

*The cata and analyses in this appendix are presented for sports enthusiasts. Although rather complicated for many Little Leaguers, they may provide an excellent opportunity for a parent-child learning experience. Source: http://www.baseball-reference.com/

Some historians have stated that William's playing record is not at the level of others in the Hall of Fame. There are certainly players with better records; however, statistics represent less than 20% of the criteria for the Hall of Fame.

It is interesting to compare William's statistics to those of other outfielders who have been elected to the Hall of Fame. Four other great outfielders (birth dates in parentheses) who have been elected to the Hall of Fame include Tommy McCarthy (1863), Max Carey (1890), Lou Brock (1939), and Ricky Henderson (1958). The data on the previous page for these four Hall of Fame players are taken from one source: *The National Baseball Hall of Fame and Museum, 2013 Yearbook*. The data for William are taken from *BASEBALL Reference.com*.

The batting averages of these players ranged from a high of 0.293 for Lou Brock to a low of 0.279 for Ricky Henderson. William's career batting average of 0.288 was in the middle of this group. Comparing Lou Brock and William Hoy's batting averages means that in 1,000 at bats, Lou would have gotten five more hits than William–that is quite close.

William's fielding percentage was above that of Tommy McCarthy. One must remember that in the days when William and Tommy played, gloves, if used at all, were very simple. So, the fielding percentages during their era (late 1800s) were considerably lower overall than in later years when gloves were much improved.

One must take care in evaluating data. To validate his accomplishments, it is helpful to compare William to these players on a more equal basis. The number of years in the Major Leagues for these players ranged from thirteen to twenty-five seasons. Therefore, one of the players had more than twice as many at bats and defensive opportunities as one of the other players.

To show an apple-to-apple comparison for these four players and William, a ratio of totals was applied. All players were compared on the equivalent basis of 7,115 at bats. For fielding/defensive statistics, all players were compared using the same number of games (1,797) as William. This is a more equal basis for looking at how much the players contributed to their teams for the analyses in the next three paragraphs.

Under this proportioned basis for the five players, William's productivity is in the upper half in most, but certainly not all, categories. Only Lou Brock (known in St. Louis as "The Franchise") and Tommy McCarthy had more hits in an equal number of at bats. William had the fewest doubles, but the most triples, on a comparable basis. Only Ricky Henderson (known as "The Man of Steal") earned more walks and accumulated more total bases than William, using the same number of at bats.

William comes in second to Tommy McCarthy in the important category of runs batted in (RBI), using an equal number of at bats. And William scored 1,429 runs, just 61 fewer runs than the leader of this important category, Ricky, when using the same number of at bats. William ranked in the middle of the five players when considering the combined number of runs batted in and the number of runs scored. Of course, the runs batted in and runs scored are particularly important, because it is the team that scores the most runs that wins the game.

On defense (playing in the field), William averaged more chances and had more putouts over the same number of games than the other four players. However, he also had more errors; this again goes back to playing without a glove or with a very early version of a glove.

Overall, William's statistics compare very favorably with the four selected greats (and a number of middle infielders) already in the Hall of Fame, when evaluated on the same number of at bats and games. While the above analyses examine just a few categories, the data clearly show that William was a highly productive player in numerous categories, both as a hitter and as a fielder.

Appendix 2
Scoring a Baseball Game

Many fans enjoy charting every play of the game on a scorecard. Over the years, a system of scoring, using shortcuts, has been developed. In this system, every fielding position is assigned a number as described in Figure 3.

For example, a ground ball double play hit to the shortstop, who throws to second base to retire a runner advancing from first base, and then the second baseman throwing to first base to retire the batter would be scored as a 6-4-3 double play. Charting a game in such a manner would have been something a person with William's intelligence and love and knowledge of the game would have enjoyed doing.

A sample scorecard is included on page 111. To learn more about scoring a baseball game, go to: www.baseballscorecard.com.

Figure 3

BASEBALL FIELD
DEFENSIVE POSITIONS

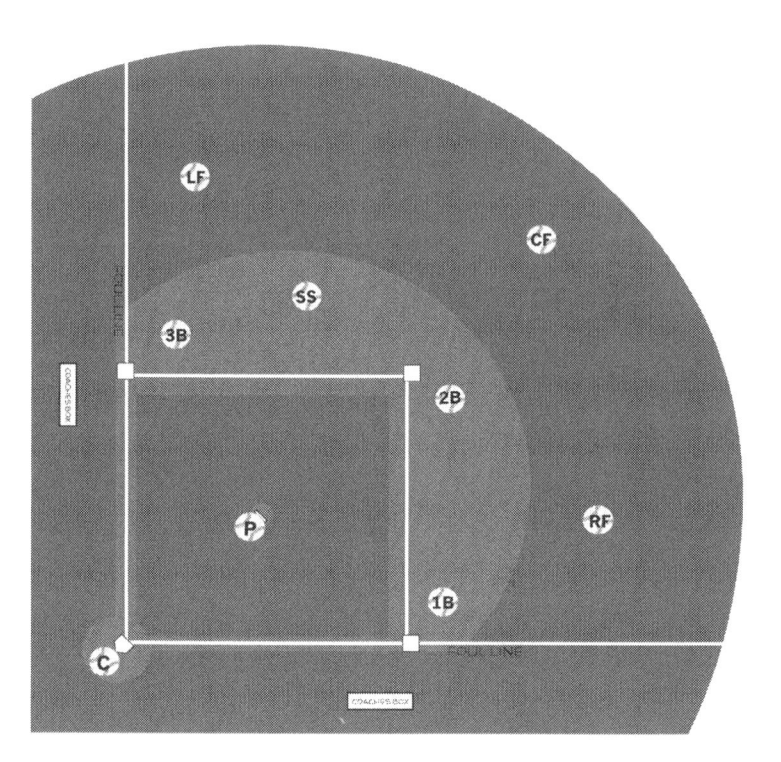

Scoring Number	Abbreviation	Position
1	P	Pitcher
2	C	Catcher
3	1B	First Base
4	2B	Second Base
5	3B	Third Base
6	SS	Short Stop
7	LF	Left Field
8	CF	Center Field
9	RF	Right Field

Figure 4

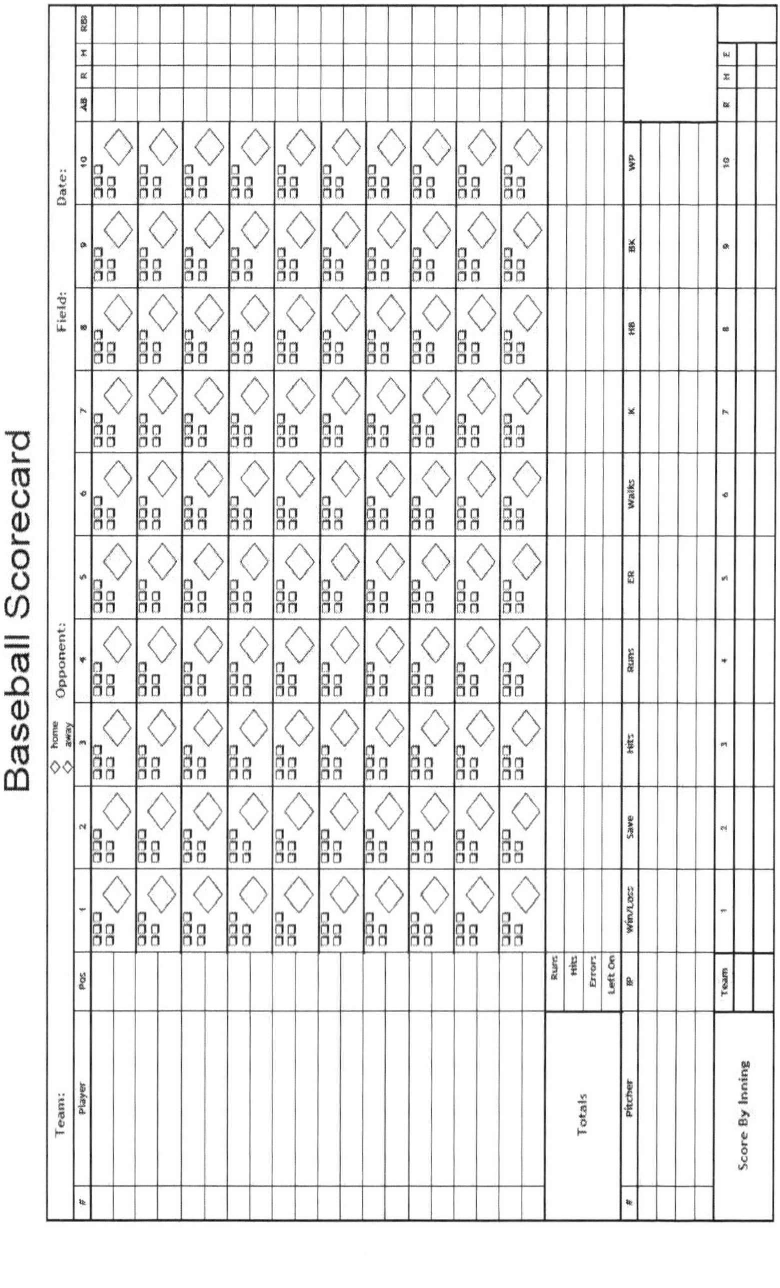
Baseball Scorecard
Team:
home
away
Opponent:
Field:
Date:
#
Player
Pos
1
2
3
4
5
6
7
8
9
10
AB
R
H
RBI
Totals
Runs
Hits
Errors
Left On
Pitcher
IP
Win/Loss
Save
Hits
Runs
ER
Walks
K
HB
BK
WP
Score By Inning
Team
R
H
E

About the Authors

Dr. Joseph Roetheli hopes that one day his epitaph (what is said about a person at the end of his or her life) will read something like this: "Loved God and family and was a creative entrepreneur and humanitarian who helped many."

What do want you want your epitaph to say?

With study and hard work, Dr. Roetheli became a successful American businessman and humanitarian. He developed the highly successful Greenies® pet treats and is the primary inventor on two other patents. Dr. Roetheli is passionate about helping others overcome challenges in life, as he has had to do himself.

Dr. Roetheli and his sister, Agnes Roetheli Gaertner, grew up on a small farm on the northern edge of the Ozark Mountains. Their parents scratched out a living. By the time the children were eight years old, they had many daily responsibilities on the farm. He and his sister, along with their brother, Alvin, grew up with very little financially, but they had loving parents and nature all about them.

Their family grew most of their own food—fruits, vegetables, and meat. Squirrel meat was often a necessity to have protein in their diet, and most of their clothes were hand-me-downs from city cousins. So, the authors truly have firsthand experience understanding the hurdles that some people face in life. They both took advantage of the opportunity to earn an education and learn from life experiences. Dr. Roetheli served his country in the U.S. Army, and Agnes spent a year in Germany as a Fullbright Foreign Exchange teacher.

Agnes Roetheli Gaertner has devoted her life to the field of education, teaching German and French at a large Southern California high school. She served as the chair of the Foreign Language Department and also of the school's Leadership Team. The really fun part of her job was coaching the students on the Academic Decathlon and Odyssey of the Mind teams, where perseverance and hard work brought home numerous awards. Her love for education continues, as she and her husband have established the Gaertner-Roetheli Scholarship at the high school in their hometown, where each year several students with interests in education, agriculture, or foreign languages are named scholarship winners. They have also built a replica one-room schoolhouse, which is stocked with era desks, books, and other classroom supplies. In addition to co-authoring this book, Mrs. Gaertner was also a part of the translation team for two books, *Nicole's Diary: Running the World… Losing Our Marbles,* by Nicole and Serge Roetheli, and *Keep on Running* by Nicole & Serge Roetheli.

Made in the USA
Coppell, TX
23 January 2020